A TRAPEZOID IS NOT A DINOSAUR!

SUZANNE MORRIS

Charlesbridge

For Faith

Published by Charlesbridge
85 Main Street • Watertown, MA 02472 • (617) 926-0329
www.charlesbridge.com

Library of Congress Cataloging-in-Publication Data
Names: Morris, Suzanne (Suzanne L.), author, illustrator.
Title: A trapezoid is not a dinosaur! / Suzanne Morris.
Description: Watertown, MA : Charlesbridge, [2019] | Summary: When Trapezoid
auditions for the Shapes in Space play, Triangle, Star, and all the other shapes insist that
his name sounds like some kind of dinosaur and that he doesn't fit in —
but Trapezoid is determined to reveal his shape properties and prove his usefulness.
Identifiers: LCCN 2018033257 (print) |
ISBN 9781580898836 (reinforced for library use) |
ISBN 9781580895804 (softcover)
LCCN 2018035947 (ebook) |
ISBN 9781632897404 (ebook) |
ISBN 9781632897411 (ebook pdf) |
Subjects: LCSH: Trapezoid—Juvenile fiction. | Shapes—Juvenile fiction. |
Humorous stories. | CYAC: Trapezoid—Fiction. | Shape—Fiction. | Humorous
stories. | LCGFT: Humorous fiction. | Picture books.
Classification: LCC PZ7.1.M6728 (ebook) | LCC PZ7.1.M6728 Tr 2019 (print) |
DDC [E]—dc23
LC record available at https://lccn.loc.gov/2018033257

Printed in China
(hc) 10 9 8 7 6 5 4 3 2 1
(sc) 10 9 8 7 6 5 4 3 2 1

Illustrations created by hand with digital assembly using graphite,
chalk, and watercolor on watercolor paper
Display and text type set in Canvas Text Sans by Yellow Design Studio
Text type set in Badger by Red Rooster Typefounders
Color separations by Colourscan Print Co Pte Ltd, Singapore
Printed by 1010 Printing International Limited in Huizhou, Guangdong, China
Production supervision by Brian G. Walker
Designed by Suzanne Morris

Showtime!

Okay, try on this costume.
You'll be the first trapezoid in space.
Really? Thank you!

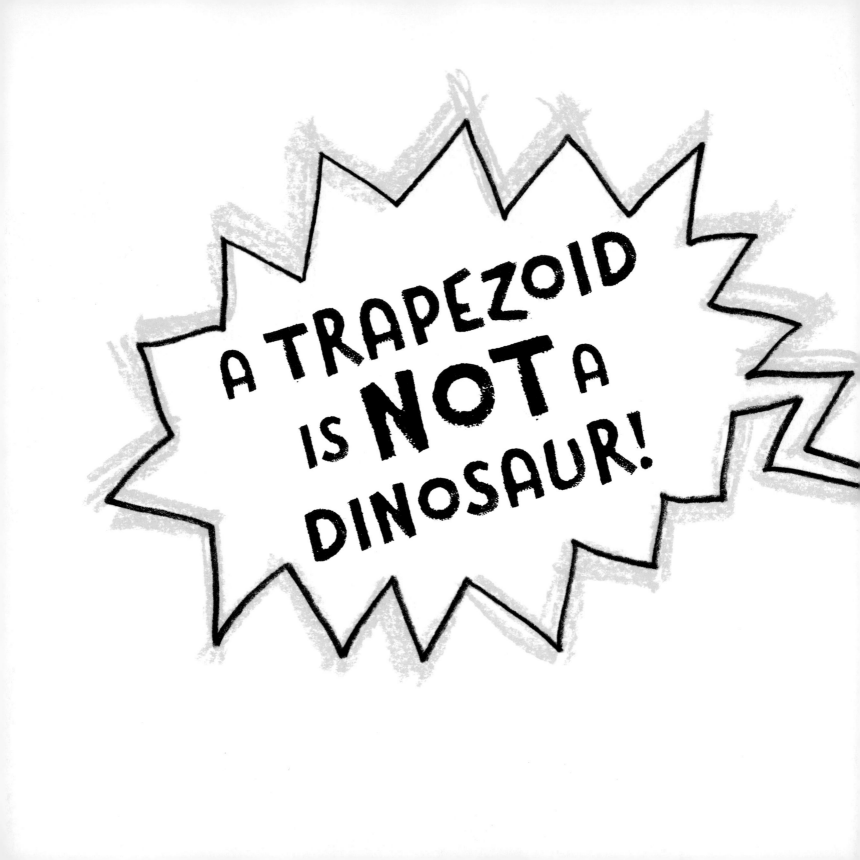

WHO'S WHO IN THE CAST

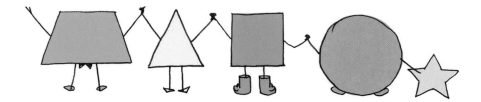

Trapezoid, Triangle, Square, Circle, and Star are all flat, closed shapes. To understand how they are alike and different, we can answer these questions about each shape:

• How many sides does the shape have?
• Is the shape made up of straight line segments or a curved line?
• Does the shape have parallel sides? If so, how many?
  (Parallel lines head in the same direction. When extended, they will never touch.)

Do you see parallel lines in the world around you? What shapes do you see? You might find trapezoids in a step stool, a takeout box, a bridge, or in the art throughout this book. There are even trapezoids in space! The four brightest stars in the Trapezium Cluster form a trapezoid. Maybe you can find this shape in the Big Dipper, too?

For more fun with shapes, visit **www.suzannemorrisart.com**.